This book
belongs to

Disney's

The Adventures of
THE GREAT MOUSE DETECTIVE

MOUSE
WORKS

Once upon a time in the kingdom of mice in England reigned a queen called Moustoria. In the year 1897 she had ruled her people for many long and happy years, and a celebration was to take place at her palace in honor of the sixtieth year of her reign.

From all corners of the world her loyal subjects flocked to the city of London to honor their beloved queen at the palace gates.

The most courageous of them was Doctor Dawson. He had traveled all the way from Afghanistan on rough and dangerous seas, fighting ferocious winds for many, many months. He arrived at last, on the eve of the celebration.

3

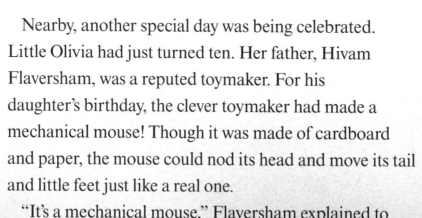

Nearby, another special day was being celebrated. Little Olivia had just turned ten. Her father, Hivam Flaversham, was a reputed toymaker. For his daughter's birthday, the clever toymaker had made a mechanical mouse! Though it was made of cardboard and paper, the mouse could nod its head and move its tail and little feet just like a real one.

"It's a mechanical mouse," Flaversham explained to the wide-eyed Olivia as he set it dancing.

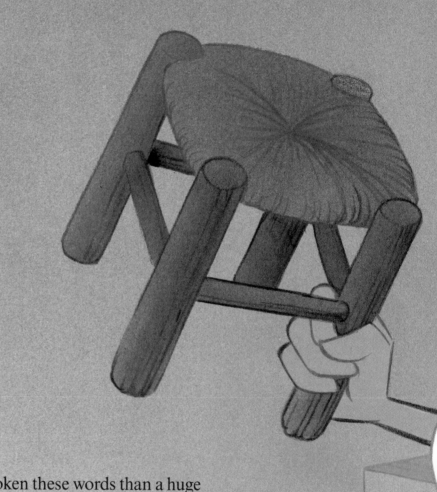

No sooner had he spoken these words than a huge shadow swept across the room. An ugly bat with enormous wings crashed in through the window.

"Hurry, Olivia! Hide in the closet!" shouted Flaversham.

Olivia quickly slipped into the closet and watched the horrifying creature grab her father and fly away with him!

Meanwhile, Doctor Dawson had taken a cab. After a few detours through the narrow streets, he called to the driver: "Let me off, please!" With his bag in one hand and his umbrella in the other, he continued his journey on foot. Somebody had told him that not too far from there he could rent a room.

As Dawson crossed the street, he saw little Olivia. She was sitting on the curb of the sidewalk, weeping.

"Why are you crying, little one?" asked Dawson.

"They took my daddy away," she sobbed, "and the only one who could ever find him and bring him back is Basil, the Great Mouse Detective."

"Basil!" said Dawson, surprised. "I was just told to go to his house to rent a room! Why don't we go there together?"

After a short walk, they reached Basil's house. It stood high on a hill in a very nice neighborhood. The housekeeper opened the door.

"Good evening, ma'am! My name is Dawson. I would like to rent a room, please."

"I'm afraid Mr. Basil isn't in yet, but he shouldn't be long. If you would like to wait, I'll make some tea," said the housekeeper. "Please come in."

Once in the house, they headed for the living room. The tea was good but they waited for Basil for a very long time. All of a sudden a figure in a long, red robe stormed into the room. In no time, off came a mask, and who appeared but … Basil! Little Olivia couldn't believe her eyes.

"To lead a successful investigation," explained the housekeeper, "Basil must go undercover. Yesterday he went out as a priest and tomorrow, well, he'll go out as a bride!"

"Tonight I'm a crack shot," Basil said, and he fired his gun. He glanced over at Dawson. "Your name is Dawson, isn't that right?" he asked. "You love pudding, but you're not too keen on walking. You just came back from Afghanistan for the queen's anniversary and you are looking for a room to rent."

"You're entirely right! How did you guess all this?" asked Dawson, taken aback.

"Elementary, my dear Dawson, that's my job," replied Basil.

16

"With that method, do you think you could find the ugly bat that took away my daddy?" asked Olivia.

"A bat?" questioned Basil. "Describe him to me!"

"He had big, bulging eyes and a wooden leg. He..."

"There is no doubt whatsoever, Olivia," interrupted Basil, "that the bat in question is Fidget!" He sat down in his armchair and lit his pipe. "Fidget is working for my archenemy Ratigan!" he continued. "Ratigan believes he should be king, but he is only a rascal! We must find his hideout and rescue your daddy as soon as possible."

Ratigan also lived in London, but in a hidden underground palace. He had gathered his subjects around his throne and was telling them his master plan.

"Everybody here knows who Queen Moustoria is," he said, holding up a picture of the queen. "I have decided to kidnap her! We need a king to rule the mice, not a queen! And that king is to be me!" Ratigan struck his chest.

"Tomorrow, at the celebration, we will make everyone believe she has chosen me as her successor!"

"And how will you do that?" asked his subjects.

"Ah! One must be very clever, indeed..." he hissed. "We shall put someone in her place!"

"Hurrah!" shouted the crowd. "Long live Ratigan!"

But Ratigan wanted more cheers, more hurrahs.
Furious, he grabbed a poor mouse out of the crowd
and summoned with a little bell, Felicia, the fat palace
cat who had a weakness for mice.

"Eat this imbecile, Felicia!" he ordered. In one
quick bite, Felicia swallowed the poor victim.

"Now you know who is the king here!" Ratigan said,
striking his chest once more.

Ratigan went to the dungeon where he held
Flaversham prisoner. "I want a mechanical mouse!"
roared the ugly rat. "Flaversham, do as I tell you, or
else..."

"Never!" cried Flaversham. "I will never betray my
beloved queen!"

"We'll see about that!" snarled Ratigan, and he left
to find Fidget the bat.

Meanwhile night had fallen on the city. Olivia and
Dawson were still at Basil's, wondering what to do.
They had agreed that nothing could be done without
first getting some evidence against Ratigan.

"Watch out!" Olivia cried out suddenly. She had caught a glimpse of Fidget outside the window, but the bat had not spotted her. "He was looking in the window, and then he turned away and walked down the street!" she told her friends.

"What a stroke of luck! Let's go outside and look for footprints," suggested Basil.

Basil was right: Fidget had left many footprints on the sidewalk.

"We can't mistake Fidget's footprints because of his wooden leg," explained Basil. But rain started to fall and the footprints disappeared one by one.

"Look here!" said Dawson, waving a cap in his hand.

"That must be Fidget's cap! He most likely dropped it as he walked," said Basil. "Good work, Dawson! It's just the piece of evidence we needed. I think I'll make you my partner, my friend!"

"Only a dog can trace the owner of this cap," said
Basil. Olivia jumped with fear.

"You needn't be scared, Olivia," said Basil. "My
friend Toby will help us find Fidget. His master is a
colleague of mine, the famous Sherlock Holmes."

When the three friends arrived at Toby's house, they
slipped in through the air vent. Toby immediately
smelled their presence. "Hello, Basil! What can I do
for you?" he asked.

"Could you sniff this cap for us?" asked Basil. "We need to find its owner, Fidget the bat."

Toby sniffed the cap several times. "Pfew! It doesn't smell very good, does it? I don't think we'll have any difficulty finding Fidget!" he exclaimed.

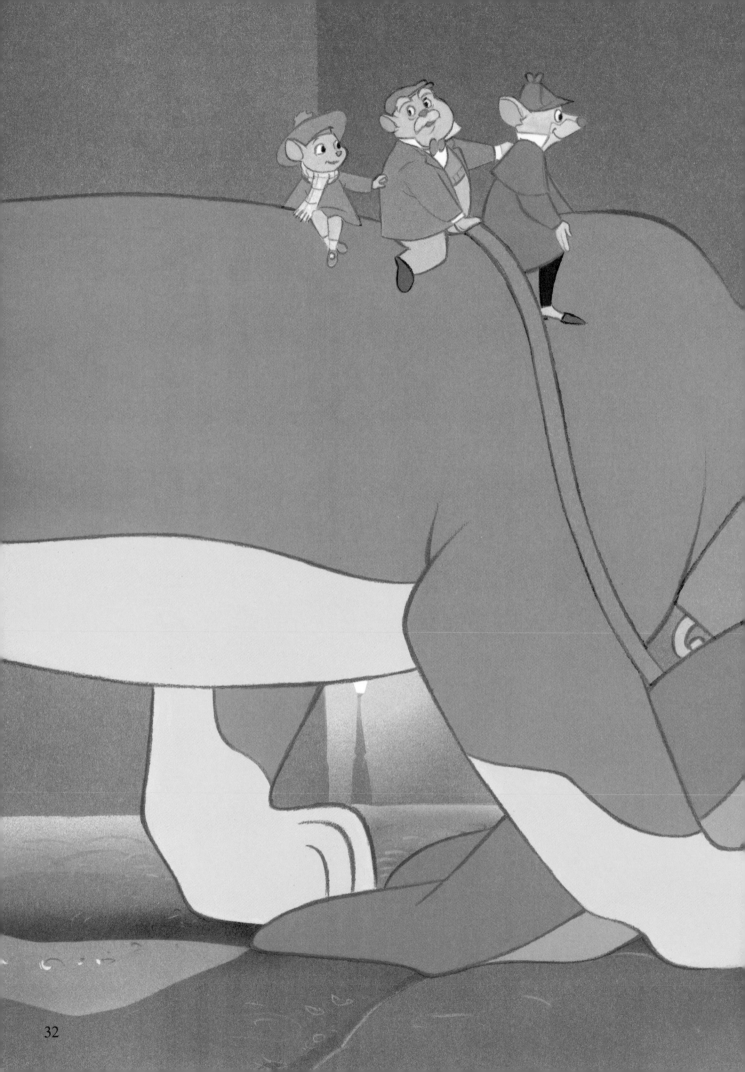

Toby followed the scent through the streets, passing squares and crossroads, with the three friends riding on his back. Finally, he stopped in front of a toy shop.

"Do you see this toy shop?" he asked, pointing. "I am absolutely positive Fidget is in there."

Toby was right. Fidget was in the store rummaging
through the toys. Ratigan had written a list of things
needed to make a mechanical mouse and Fidget was
now stealing all the straps, pulleys, screws and caps
that were necessary.

The wicked bat was also stealing uniforms off toy
soldiers, too small for human beings to wear, but a
perfect fit for mice!

Basil, Dawson and Olivia wasted no time. Toby opened a window and the three friends slipped inside the shop. Toby was too big to follow them. "Good luck!" he whispered to them before he left.

But Fidget had very good ears. He overheard Toby and quickly hid in a row of toys.

"Where on earth has he gone?" wondered Basil aloud, as they looked around the shop.

"Very strange indeed," whispered Dawson. "But there is something even stranger: None of these toy soldiers has any clothes!"

Olivia answered with a scream. She had spotted Fidget behind some toys.

Basil and Dawson were so startled by her scream that they stopped dead in their tracks. Fidget grabbed Olivia and shoved her in his bag. Before anything could be done, the bat had escaped with Olivia through a hole in the roof.

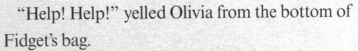

"Help! Help!" yelled Olivia from the bottom of
Fidget's bag.

"Don't worry, Olivia! We'll rescue you!" shouted
back Basil. He dashed up a pile of wooden blocks in
pursuit of Fidget. Dawson charged after him but before
either could reach the top, the whole pile tumbled
down on top of them!

Fidget took Olivia directly to Ratigan. The cruel rat brought her down to the dungeon where her father was held prisoner.

"Aren't they adorable?" he hissed as father and daughter hugged. Raising his voice to a roar, he threatened Flaversham: "You are cornered, Flaversham! If you don't do as I tell you, I'll have Felicia feast on your darling daughter. Now, start working!"

Torn by Ratigan's threats, Flaversham started to work on the mechanical mouse.

Meanwhile, in the shop, the great Basil had far from given up. As soon as he recovered from his fall, he picked up the list Fidget had dropped, and carefully began to examine it.

"My dear Dawson, everything one needs to know is on this list," explained Basil, "but only for those who know how to see. With a careful examination I can tell you where it came from, where it's been and who's held it. We'll soon know where Ratigan is hiding!"

Ratigan had no trust in Flaversham and decided to keep Olivia as a hostage. "Fidget!" he bellowed. "Put Olivia in this bottle! If this little crybaby escapes, I'll have Felicia feast on you instead!"

"But Your Majesty, what have I done?" whined Fidget.

"You lost the list, didn't you, you fool? I think I'll have you punished right now." With great pleasure, Ratigan shook his little bell to call Felicia.

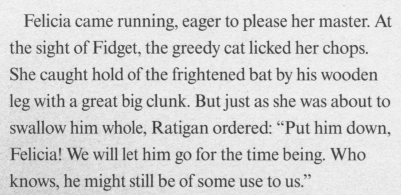

Felicia came running, eager to please her master. At the sight of Fidget, the greedy cat licked her chops. She caught hold of the frightened bat by his wooden leg with a great big clunk. But just as she was about to swallow him whole, Ratigan ordered: "Put him down, Felicia! We will let him go for the time being. Who knows, he might still be of some use to us."

Felicia reluctantly let her prey go, with a disappointed groan.

That night, disguised as a captain and his roguish first mate, Basil and Dawson went to one of the sailors' bars on the harbor.

"Let's sit down, Dawson," whispered Basil. "If Ratigan lives nearby as we suspect, someone here will no doubt mention him. Let's listen carefully!"

The sailors were singing a very catchy tune, and
Dawson, a little tipsy, wanted to join them. Singing
along, he jumped on the piano and in no time a fight
broke out in the barroom. Hats, shoes, chairs, tables,
and even the piano were flying across the room! What
a mess!

But Basil, undaunted, slipped behind the counter and called out to Dawson to follow him. "Something tells me that Fidget escaped through here," he said, lifting a trap door. "Soon we will catch up with him!"

Basil and Dawson lowered themselves into the
opening, then followed a flight of stairs down to the
city sewers. The old walls of the port reeked a horrible
stench, and they could not see anything in the pitch
dark.

"Be careful!" warned Dawson. "It's very slippery!"

"Quiet!" whispered Basil. "Over there! Did you see Fidget standing in that doorway?" Basil pointed to a ray of light. "How strange! It looked as if Fidget wanted us to see him!" Slowly they crept towards the door.

In their excitement, Basil and Dawson threw caution to the wind. They opened the door and saw Olivia trapped in the bottle. Before they could free her, they were surrounded by Ratigan's guards.

"Rats!" exclaimed Basil. "It's a trap! What a fool I am! I should have guessed this was a trick!"

"You are right, my dear Basil," snickered Ratigan, as guards bound Basil and Dawson with ropes. "You are indeed a fool. Even geniuses make mistakes! I, for instance, expected you at half past eight and it's only twenty past. But you arrived just in time to celebrate a marvelous little invention of which I am very proud," he continued with a wicked smile.

"Be a good sport, my dear friend," said Ratigan, wringing his hands with pleasure. "Wouldn't you like to know how this ingenious mousetrap works? It's a true work of art! Oh, but you don't look too comfortable, do you? It's a little too tight? I am so sorry. Don't be too upset, your worries will soon be over!" With that, Ratigan broke into hideous laughter.

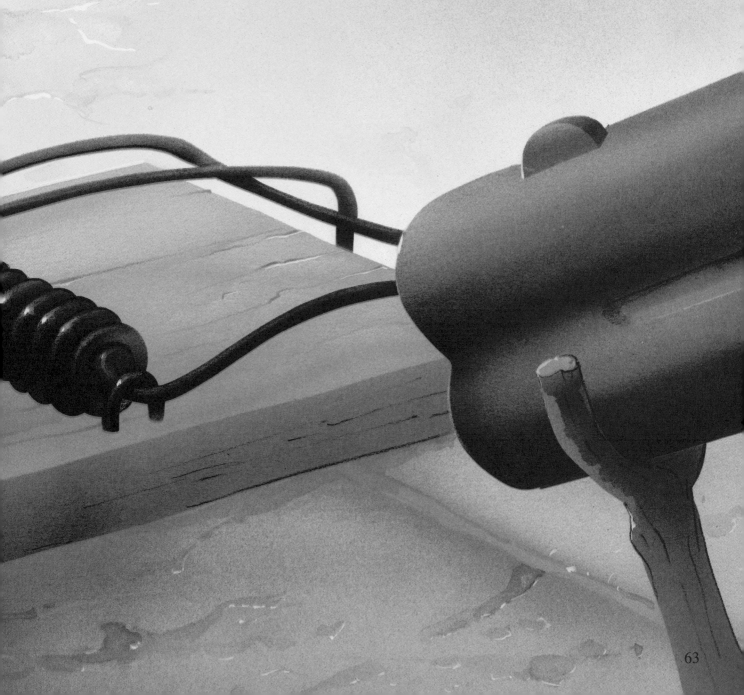

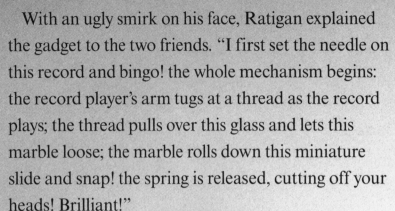

With an ugly smirk on his face, Ratigan explained the gadget to the two friends. "I first set the needle on this record and bingo! the whole mechanism begins: the record player's arm tugs at a thread as the record plays; the thread pulls over this glass and lets this marble loose; the marble rolls down this miniature slide and snap! the spring is released, cutting off your heads! Brilliant!"

"And just to be on the safe side," he continued, "this crossbow will shoot you as the trap is released, the axe will chop you in half and the anvil will crush you to pieces!"

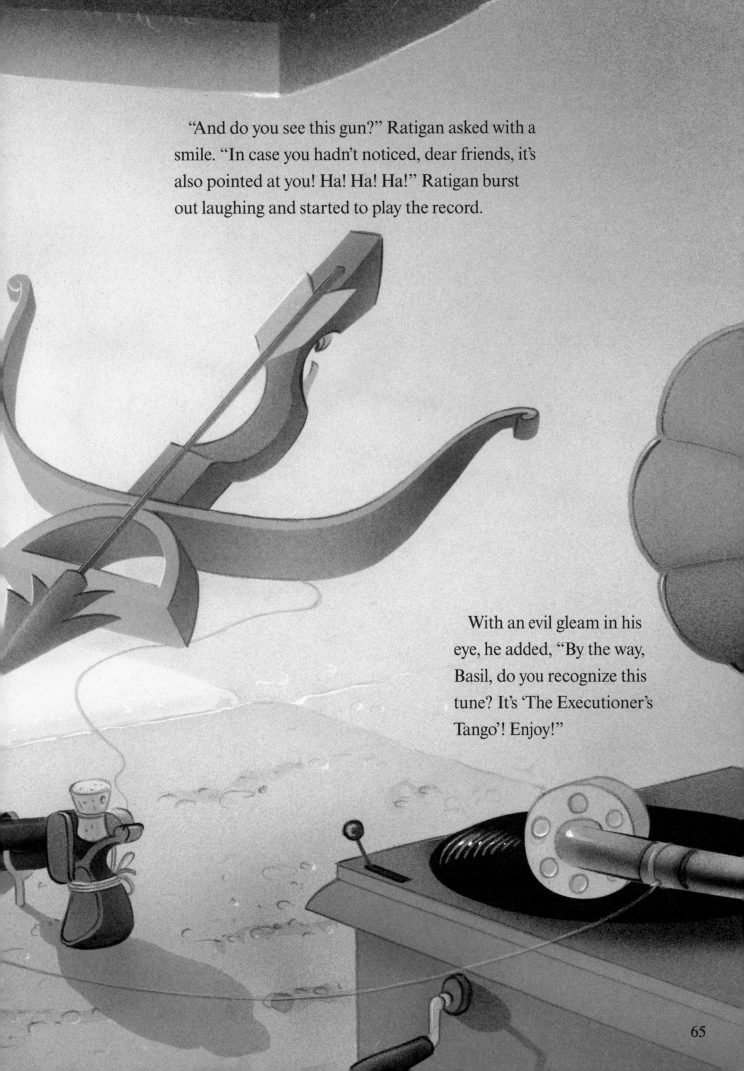

"And do you see this gun?" Ratigan asked with a smile. "In case you hadn't noticed, dear friends, it's also pointed at you! Ha! Ha! Ha!" Ratigan burst out laughing and started to play the record.

With an evil gleam in his eye, he added, "By the way, Basil, do you recognize this tune? It's 'The Executioner's Tango'! Enjoy!"

While Basil and Dawson were in this terrible predicament, Queen Moustoria received an enormous gift ... from Ratigan.

"Oh, my!" she exclaimed as she opened it. "A full-size replica of me! What a thoughtful gift! This Ratigan is a true gentleman!"

To the queen's surprise the statue started to move. "Kings and queens have had small and large statues of themselves, but never have I heard of a moving statue. How delightful!" said the queen as she moved closer to examine it. She did not see Ratigan in the adjoining room, operating the statue.

"Get hold of her!" shouted Ratigan at the queen's two guards.

The queen couldn't believe her eyes. "What! My own soldiers! Stop!" she yelled in vain. Little did she know that these were not her soldiers, but Ratigan's accomplices dressed with the costumes Fidget had stolen from the toy shop!

"Wasn't it a brilliant idea to steal these uniforms, Fidget?" asked the delighted Ratigan.

"But I was the one to carry out your idea," said Fidget.

"Shut up, you bat!" snarled Ratigan.

Without another word, Fidget picked up the Queen and carried her away like a bag of potatoes.

Back in Ratigan's secret chamber, Basil had an idea. "Our only chance is to release the spring before this dreadful music comes to an end. Let me think ... Dawson, when I tell you, kick as hard as you can!"

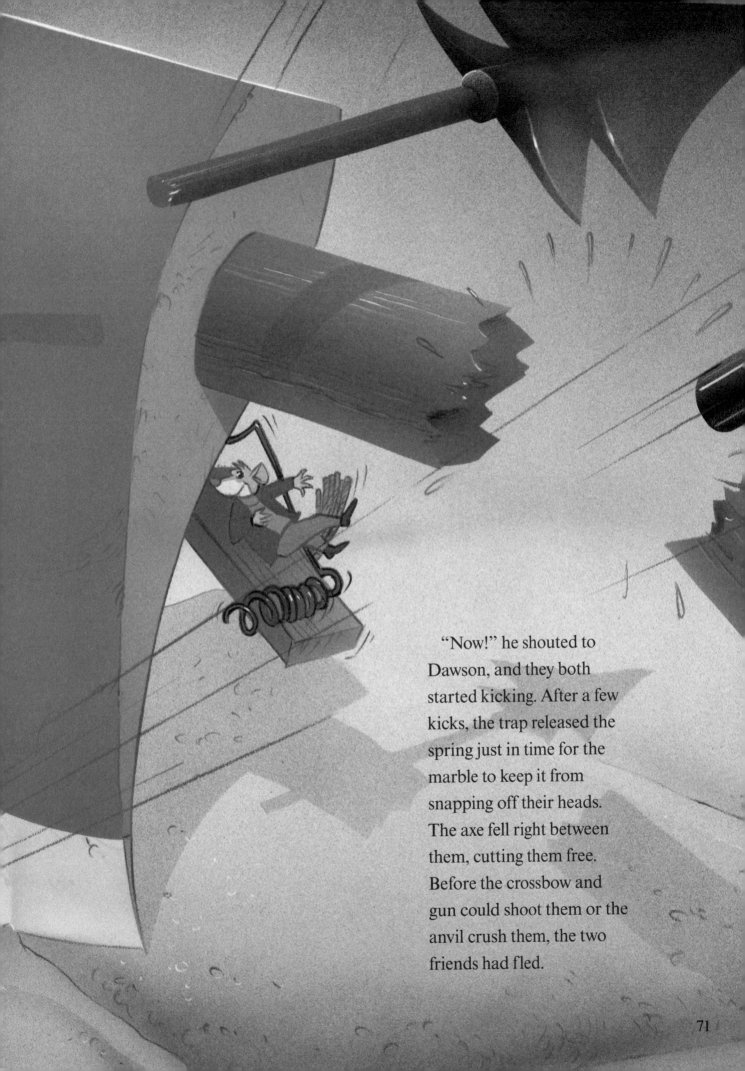

"Now!" he shouted to Dawson, and they both started kicking. After a few kicks, the trap released the spring just in time for the marble to keep it from snapping off their heads. The axe fell right between them, cutting them free. Before the crossbow and gun could shoot them or the anvil crush them, the two friends had fled.

Basil and Dawson rushed to free Olivia from inside the bottle. They found Toby, who had tracked them down, and rode on his back to the queen's palace as quickly as they could.

At the palace, Fidget was about to throw Queen Moustoria into Felicia's hungry mouth. With a quick jump Basil caught hold of the queen, while Toby, with a formidable roar, chased a terrified Felicia out of the palace. The queen was saved!

Meanwhile, in the palace's meeting hall, the fake queen was addressing her people: "My loyal subjects, after sixty years of ruling I am old enough to be a grandmother. Instead, I have found my true love and will remarry. Ratigan will soon become my husband. As a wedding gift, I wish him to reign in my place."

The crowd could not see Flaversham behind the stage, forced by Ratigan to operate the mechanical mouse!

Ratigan entered the stage in a sumptuous royal robe. He smiled triumphantly at the crowd, waiting for their applause. But they had recognized him and shrunk back in terror. They knew that the chosen husband of their queen would not address them kindly.

"I, Ratigan the First," he shouted, "King of the Mice, hereby declare that a heavy tax shall be paid by all spongers such as the elderly, the infirm, and especially, little children!"

Just as Ratigan finished his cruel speech, Basil, Dawson, Flaversham and Olivia ran out onto the stage. "Listen everybody!" Basil shouted, "Ratigan is an impostor!" With one swift kick from Basil, the mechanical mouse fell to pieces.

The crowd was furious. "This fat rat is a liar! Let's get him!"

Everyone rushed to the stage. But Ratigan was quick as lightning. He swooped down, grabbed hold of little Olivia and escaped before anyone could catch him!

Ratigan had thought of everything! Outside the palace gates a small dirigible was waiting for him in case something went wrong. He pushed Olivia into the gondola and soon they were flying up toward the clouds!

"He fooled us!" sighed Dawson. Flaversham nodded sadly in agreement. But Basil was already hard at work building a second dirigible, out of wooden planks, children's balloons and the queen's flag. In no time, they were flying up into the sky in pursuit of Ratigan.

With the next gust of wind they caught up with Ratigan's dirigible.

"There is only one solution: I've got to jump into their gondola!" said Basil.

"But that's impossible!" cried Flaversham.

"He's right. You can't possibly do that!" seconded Dawson.

But Basil had already jumped. He landed right next to Ratigan who was so surprised that he let go of the dirigible's steering wheel!

"Watch out, the clock tower!" shouted Dawson and Flaversham, but it was too late....

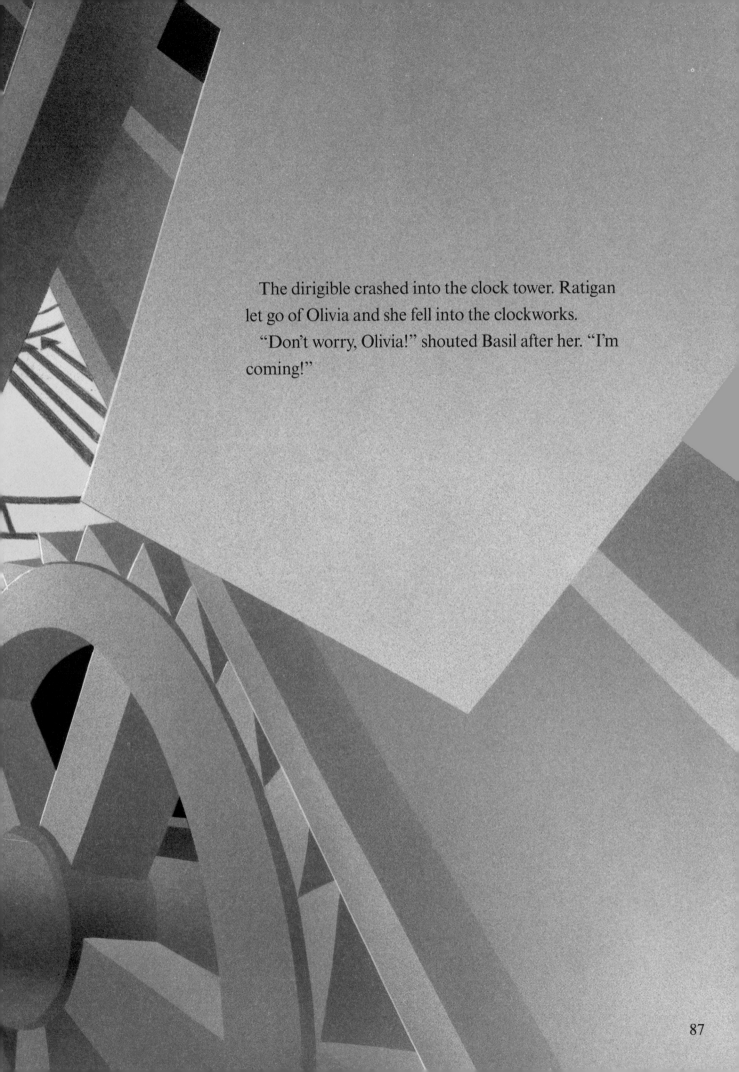

The dirigible crashed into the clock tower. Ratigan let go of Olivia and she fell into the clockworks.

"Don't worry, Olivia!" shouted Basil after her. "I'm coming!"

Grabbing hold of a rope, Basil swung to where Olivia had fallen. He tied the rope around her and with a strong push he swung her to her father in the dirigible. Little Olivia was finally safe in her father's arms!

But Basil's troubles were not yet over. Ratigan was furious. He threw himself at Basil with the force of a wild tiger. Basil jumped to the side and struck his enemy over the head. Ratigan turned around and snarled, "You imbecile detective! Wait until I get my hands on you!"

But Basil had already thought of a plan to trick Ratigan. He moved back on the clock's big hand hoping Ratigan would follow him there.

Suddenly the clock struck the hour. DONG! DONG! DONG! The whole tower shook with the sound. Basil had held on tight to the clock hand, but, just as he expected, Ratigan was taken by surprise. The ugly rat lost his balance and catapulted off the clock hand into the void.

Basil leaped off the tower into the dirigible and joined his friends.

"How can I ever thank you enough?" Queen Moustoria said when the four friends returned to the palace. "You saved my country and me from a most horrible and cruel rat! Thank you."

But Basil wanted to thank Dawson for his help. "My dear Dawson," he said with a smile, "without your help, I wouldn't have been able to save the kingdom of mice from the scoundrel Ratigan." But that wasn't all Basil had to say. "How would you like to become my associate, Dawson?" he asked, holding out his hand.

"I was hoping you would ask me," Dawson replied.

And with a strong handshake, the world's most famous detective team was formed: Basil the Great Mouse Detective and Doctor Dawson.

ISBN 1-57082-039-2
10 9 8 7 6 5 4 3 2